Humpty Dumpty

Abby's friend Humpty sat on a wall,
but Abby's friend Humpty had a great fall.
Poor Humpty Dumpty, what will he do?
It's Abby Cadabby to the rescue!

Abby waves her wand and casts a spell,
but will it work? No one can tell!

"Leg, beg, diddle-diddle deg, reg, EGG!"

Poof!

Oh dear, Abby's spell didn't work!

Abby tries again—
this spell is new.
She's sure it will work.
Do you think so, too?

"Len, ben, diddle-diddle den.
Turn Humpty into a whole egg AGAIN!"

"I said WHOLE EGG AGAIN, not A HEN!"
says Abby. "Hmm, let's try something non-magical."

Abby calls all the King's horses and all the King's men
to help put Humpty together again.

But all the King's horses and all the King's men
couldn't put Humpty together again!

Abby had one more idea of her own:
"I'll just use a little tape and some glue
and soon Humpty Dumpty will be good as new!"

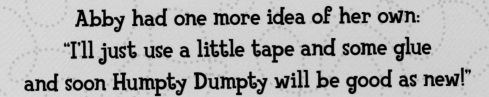

HUMPTY DUMPTY

Humpty Dumpty sat on a wall.
Humpty Dumpty had a great fall.
All the King's horses and all the King's men
couldn't put Humpty together again.

The Old Woman Who Lived in a Shoe

Abby knows an old woman
who lives in a shoe.
She has so many children,
what can she do?
It's Abby Cadabby
to the rescue!

Abby waves her wand and casts a spell.
But will it work? No one can tell!

"Town, zown, diddle-diddle gown.
Kids, please settle DOWN!"

"I said SETTLE DOWN,
not CLOWN IN A GOWN!" says Abby.
"There must be a problem with spell
reception today. I'll try a different one."

Abby tries again—
this one is new.
She's sure it will work.
Do you think so, too?

Poof!

"Leep, keep, diddle-diddle reep.
Children please go to SLEEP!"

"I said SLEEP, not SHEEP!" says Abby.
"Oh, I give up. What else would work?"
Abby decides to give the old woman some advice

"Maybe they just need a snack,
before they're tucked in tight.
And I always need a kiss
just to say good night."

Poof!

THE OLD WOMAN WHO LIVED IN A SHOE

There was an old woman
who lived in a shoe,
she had so many children,
she didn't know what to do.
She gave them some broth
and a piece of bread,
kissed them all gently,
and put them to bed.

Mary Had a Little Lamb

Abby's friend Mary had a little lamb
who followed her to school one day.
It was against the rules.
What will Mary do?
It's Abby Cadabby to the rescue!

Abby waves her wand and casts a spell.
But will it work? No one can tell!

"Bide, fide, diddle-diddle pide.
Lamb, you now must go OUTSIDE!"

Oh dear, Abby's spell didn't work!

"I guess I need more practice! I'll try it again."

Abby tries again—
this spell is new.
She's sure it will work.
Do you think so, too?

Poof!

"Bool, zool, diddle-diddle spool.

Lamb, you must leave this SCHOOL!"

"I said leave SCHOOL, not POOL!" says Abby.
"I guess I still have a lot to learn about spells."

Abby has an idea for Mary and her teacher:

"I like to play outside. Maybe if you take
your lamb out to the playground it will
play until you're done with school!"

MARY HAD A LITTLE LAMB

Mary had a little lamb.
Its fleece was white as snow.
And everywhere that Mary went,
the lamb was sure to go.

It followed her to school one day,
which was against the rules.
It made the children laugh and play,
to see a lamb at school.

And so the teacher turned it out,
but still it lingered near.
And waited patiently about,
till Mary did appear.

"Why does the lamb love Mary so?"
The eager children cry.
"Why, Mary loves the lamb, you know."
The teacher did reply.